My Hippopotamus is on Our Caravan Roof Getting Sunburnt

My HIPPOPOTAMUS
is on Our Caravan Roof
Getting Sunburnt

by Hazel Edwards

illustrated by Deborah Niland

PUFFIN BOOKS

For James
D.N.

PUFFIN BOOKS

Published by the Penguin Group
Penguin Group (Australia)
707 Collins Street,
Melbourne, Victoria 3008, Australia
(a division of Pearson Australia Group Pty Ltd)
Penguin Group (USA) Inc.
375 Hudson Street, New York, New York 10014, USA
Penguin Group (Canada)
90 Eglinton Avenue East, Suite 700, Toronto, ON M4P 2Y3, Canada
(a division of Pearson Penguin Canada Inc.)
Penguin Books Ltd
80 Strand, London WC2R 0RL, England
Penguin Ireland
25 St Stephen's Green, Dublin 2, Ireland
(a division of Penguin Books Ltd)
Penguin Books India Pvt Ltd
11, Community Centre, Panchsheel Park, New Delhi-110 017, India
Penguin Group (NZ)
67 Apollo Drive, Rosedale, Auckland 0632, New Zealand
(a division of Pearson New Zealand Ltd)
Penguin Books (South Africa) (Pty) Ltd
181 Jan Smuts Avenue, Park Town North, Johannesburg 2196, South Africa
Penguin (Beijing) Ltd,
7F, Tower B, Jiaming Centre, 27 East Third Ring Road North,
Chaoyang District, Beijing 100020, China

Penguin Books Ltd, Registered Offices: 80 Strand, London, WC2R 0RL, England

First published by Hodder Headline Australia Pty Ltd, 1989
This edition reissued by Penguin Group (Australia), 2006

7 9 10 8 6

Text copyright © Hazel Edwards, 1989
Illustrations copyright © Deborah Niland, 1989

The moral right of the author and illustrator has been asserted

Offset from the Hodder Headline edition
Printed and bound in China by Everbest Printing Co. Ltd.

National Library of Australia
Cataloguing-in-Publication data:

Edwards, Hazel, 1945- .
My hippopotamus is on our caravan roof getting sunburnt.

978 0 14 350138 1

1. Hippopotamus - Juvenile fiction. I. Niland, Deborah.
II. Title.

A823.3

puffin.com.au

Our family went on a holiday.
Pack.
Unpack.
Pack again.
We'd never stayed at the beach before.

There's a hippopotamus on our roof eating cake.
I wanted him to go too.
My daddy said, 'We can't take everything.'
But my hippopotamus packed his cake.

Click.
Click.
Click.
We put on our seatbelts.
And drove for hours and hours.
I threw up. It was awful.
My hippopotamus doesn't get carsick.
There's a hippopotamus on the roof of our car eating cake.

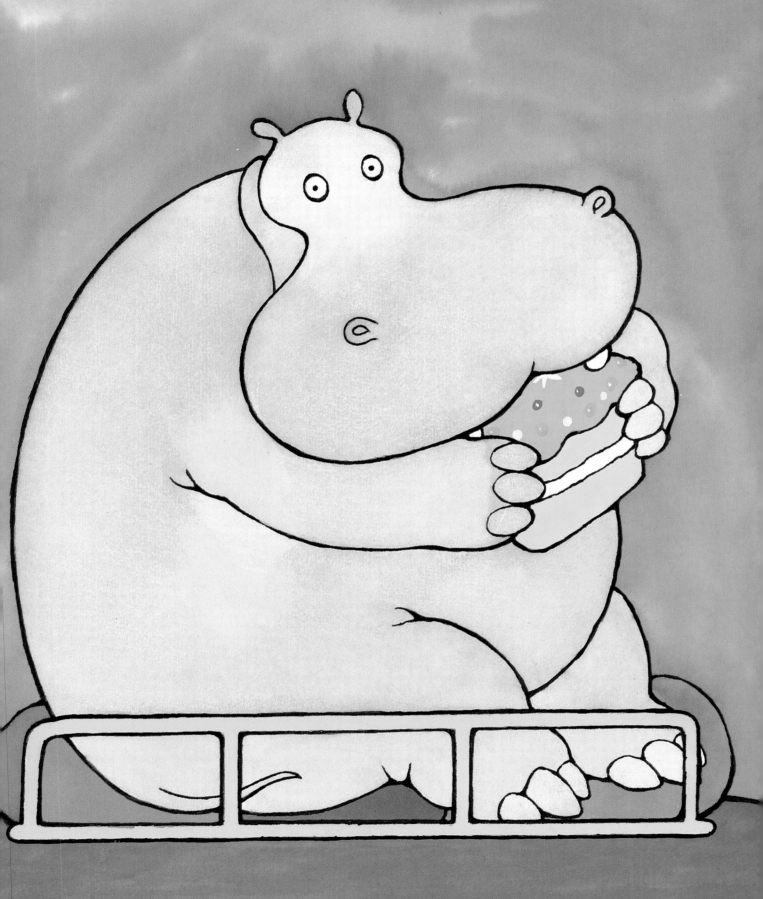

'There's the beach!'
Daddy took a photograph.
I wanted a photograph of my hippopotamus.
But Daddy said he might be too big to fit in the picture.

It was very hot at the beach.
Mummy wore sunglasses.
Daddy wore a floppy hat.
We all wore T-shirts.

We played in the rock pools and collected shells.
Then we went for a swim.
'Don't go out too far,' Mummy said.
My hippopotamus can swim anywhere.
He floats really well.

Lunch was under the beach umbrella.
Mummy had salad.
Daddy had cheese and pickles.
My big brother and I had meat sandwiches.
My hippopotamus had cake and he didn't quite fit under
   the umbrella.

We made sandcastles in the wet sand.
'You're getting sunburnt,' said Daddy. 'You'll have to be careful.'
My hippopotamus got sunburnt too.
Now he's standing on the roof eating cake

We all went fishing on the pier.
But we only caught one fish.
My hippopotamus caught hundreds.
There's a hippopotamus on our caravan roof eating fish.

'Something stinks,' said Mummy.
'It's those shells,' said Daddy. 'Throw them away.'
My hippopotamus can collect anything.
Nobody throws out his shell collection.

'There's something on the roof,' whispered Mummy in
the middle of the night.
Thump.
Thump.
Thump.
'It's only a possum,' said Daddy.
I know it's my hippopotamus.
There's a hippopotamus on our caravan roof in a
sleeping bag.

On the sand, we played cricket.
I missed the ball.
'You're out,' said my brother.
My hippopotamus could bowl him out first ball.

We rode the waves on our kickboards.
I kept falling off.
My brother is a good surfer.
There's a hippopotamus on a surfboard making waves.

No more sand.
No more sea.
No more sun.
We came home today.
There are lots of holiday photographs.
My hippopotamus is too shy for photographs.
He's back on the roof.

There's a hippopotamus on our roof, eating cake.